Acknowledging

Meirion

By

Zenobia Renquist

This is a work of fiction. Names, characters, places, and incidents are products of the author's imagination or are used fictitiously and are not to be construed as real. Any resemblance to actual events, locales, organizations, or persons, living or dead, is entirely coincidental.

Acknowledging Meirion By Zenobia Renquist

Red Rose™ Publishing
Publishing with a touch of Class! ™
The symbol of the Red Rose and Red Rose is a trademark of Red Rose™ Publishing

Red Rose™ Publishing
Copyright© 2009 Zenobia Renquist
ISBN: 978-1-60435-918-3
ISBN: 1-60435-918-8
Cover Artist: Elizabeth Chesterman
Editor: Mike
Line Editor:

Red Rose™ Publishing
www.redrosepublishing.com
Forestport, NY 13338

Thank you for purchasing a book from Red Rose™ Publishing where publishing comes with a touch of Class!

Chapter One

Meirion shut off the shower and waited.

Nothing happened.

She shook her head. "Must be hearing things."

She reached for the hot water nozzle when a faint thumping reached her ears. Someone was knocking at her door. "Damn it. He's early. He should know better than to show up to a woman's house for a date early. Idiot," she grumbled as she climbed out the shower, wrapped herself in a towel and trudged out of the bathroom.

The knocking got louder and more urgent.

"I'm coming, damn it. Hold on." She glared behind her. "It'd be a great help if one of you guys could get the door."

No answer, just a blank stare. She didn't know why she bothered talking to the men. They never said anything.

She yanked open the door, ready to lay in to her boyfriend for showing up early but he wasn't the one standing on the other side.

"Who are you and what do you want?"

The nervous looking teen fidgeted as he tried to think of what to say.

"I just climbed out of a warm shower to answer this door. You better have a damn good reason for disturbing me."

"I...uh...well, that is...my buddies and I—"

"Spit it out already!"

"You've got a Fey in there, right? You're one of the ones being watched, right? My buddies said they saw them come out of your house the other day. I just wanted to see one. Please?" He peered over her shoulder trying to see inside the house.

Meirion forced a fake smile. She was used to this. Ever

since the Fey put her under surveillance, everyone around her was curious to see and talk to them. She'd had her shadows for two years and the Fey had lived on Earth for five. People should be used to them by now, but no. Idiots like the one on her doorstep still existed.

She said in a sweet voice, "I'm not dressed for company, otherwise I'd let you in."

"Yeah, I'm sorry about that. I saw your car in the drive—"

"If you just wait here, I'll get dressed and be right back. Okay?"

"You mean it?"

"Sure do. Stay right here. I won't be long." She closed the door and rolled her eyes. "Putz." She went to the kitchen, picked up the phone and dialed the cops. They received so many calls from her in the last two years that they'd given her a direct line.

"Evening, Ms. Flatt, is this a social call?"

"Got another one for you, Tony."

"That's what I thought. I'll have Sam and Fred out there in no time. Front porch?"

"Standing there like a dope, as usual. I can't believe the dumb ass really thinks I'll let him in my house. Since I know he won't leave if left to his own cognizance, I thought the police could help him along."

"That's what we're here for."

"Tell Sam and Fred I said thanks."

"Will do, have a good night."

Meirion hung up the phone and waited. Not ten minutes later, a patrol car siren filtered through her windows. She went to the front door and peeked out the side window. Sam and Fred had arrived and were carting away her nosy teen, who fought them the whole way.

She opened her door and watched with a smile on her

face, genuine this time. "That never gets old." She leaned against the doorjamb. Movement behind her made her glance over her shoulder. One of her shadows had come up behind her so he could watch the teen be shoved into the back of the patrol car and driven away.

"You guys are a pain in my ass, I hope you know that. Following me all the time isn't giving you an accurate representation of my life since people act funny around you."

The man didn't answer.

In fact, he wouldn't answer. In the two years she'd lived with the three Fey, none of them had said word one to her. They weren't allowed. Their job was to film her, that's it. She was a participant in the human version of a nature show and the viewers on a different planet were light years away.

She had three "cameramen" and they watched her on

ten-hour shifts. Night or day, awake or asleep, at home or out—they watched her every move unless she was using the toilet. The home viewers weren't interested in human waste disposal. Hiding on the toilet was her only option for privacy and she used it. She wasn't the only one. Several of the other observees did the same when they realized their shadows wouldn't follow them and watch.

Sam and Fred waved at her and she closed the door. A quick glance at the cable box clock showed she had fifteen minutes until Allen's arrival. He'd better be on time too. She was supposed to make him wait not vice versa.

She glanced at the clock again. Three more hours and Kiar would arrive for his shift. While all of the Fey were good looking, she thought Kiar was the most handsome one she'd ever seen.

Her co-workers felt Eiliv, her current shadow, was the better looking of the three she'd gotten. They only liked his silver hair. The man had silver growing out of his head and it flowed down his back to his calves. He wore it in a long braid at all times. She'd never seen him take it down.

The silver complimented his dark purple skin and deep, true blue eyes. Actually, his eyes changed colors, going from true blue to dark blue. Meirion had yet to figure out a pattern or if it was based on emotions or what. She couldn't ask since he wouldn't answer.

She checked the impulse to tweak the man's long, pointed ears. It was a constant urge whenever she looked at a Fey's ears. The points extended well above the tops of their heads and she'd been curious of their flexibility since the first time she saw a Fey. She wondered if heavy earrings would make their ears droop.

Eiliv stared at her with his unblinking gaze as she looked him over. She said with a mischievous grin, "One of these days I'm going to shave you bald and cash your hair in for a new car."

One more glance at the clock. "But not today." She rushed back to her room with Eiliv following.

She yanked off her towel and tossed it into the bathroom then went in search of the perfect panty and bra set to go with her off-the-shoulder, knee-length party dress.

Being naked in front of Eiliv didn't bother her. Neither did the idea of thousands of home viewers seeing her naked. They were all Fey. No one on Earth got to see the footage her shadows recorded. It had taken her a year to get used to them watching her in the shower. Their lack of reaction helped.

She stopped noticing them after a while and went on with her life. That didn't stop her from teasing them every now and then. Someone told her she'd get the guards at Buckingham palace to talk before a Fey shadow. While true, that didn't stop her from trying.

"What do you think? The blue or the green?" She held one bra in front of her chest and then the other.

Eiliv said nothing and gave no outward reaction.

She turned to the mirror and did the swap again. "I don't even know why it matters since Allen won't see them anyway."

But Kiar will, said a little voice in the back of her head.

"Green," she answered herself.

To match Kiar's hair. How cute. You've been wearing a lot of green lately.

She ignored her inner teasing and finished dressing.

Allen arrived right on time. Meirion sat him on her bed while she styled her hair. "Where are we going?" she called.

"A club I found. Great music and fantastic food."

"I'm not overdressed, am I?"

"You're perfect," he replied near her bathroom door.

She looked at him and he smiled at her.

Allen was an old friend from her college days. He'd admitted to having a crush on her way back then but didn't want to make her choose between her then boyfriend and him.

Ten years later, Allen had matured in personality and looks. He wore his brown hair in a short cut instead of a disheveled, shoulder-length mass. He'd traded too-big jeans that rode his hips and baggy shirts for the corporate suit-and-tie image.

Even when he dressed down, like now, his jeans stayed at his waist and his shirts fit. He liked showing off the muscular physique his personal trainer helped him achieve, so the baggy clothes were out.

"So..."

"So?"

"Is tall, dark and shiny tagging along too?" he asked.

"Of course, Allen. You knew that already. Actually, Eiliv should only be with us for the first part of the night. Kiar takes over in another three hours."

"Great."

Meirion turned away from the mirror and looked at him. "What's with you? You know I can't go anywhere without them."

"I didn't figure they'd follow you to a crowded club."

"Is that why you picked a club?" She laughed and shook her head. "Nice try, but it won't work. I'm not losing them. I've tried."

"They just creep me out. Have you ever seen them blink?"

"Nope. They don't because of the camera in their left eye. If they blink, then that's a second of footage they lose."

"I've heard the Fey that don't have cameras don't blink either. How the hell do you go through the day and not

13

blink?"

"That's their species, Allen. Their eyes work different than ours. Just leave it at that and stop obsessing over crap you can't change. He's coming and you can't get rid of him."

"We're taking my car."

"Is that because mine has a camera?"

He didn't answer but Meirion knew she'd guessed right. She put the finishing touches on her hair then turned to Allen. "Let's go."

The trio stepped out of the house and Meirion locked the door. Once at Allen's car, Meirion got in and Eiliv disappeared—literally. Allen's look turned satisfied.

Meirion didn't have the heart to tell him Eiliv wasn't gone. He'd teleported to the Fey ship while Allen drove Meirion to wherever and then Eiliv would reappear. His disappearance also meant Allen's car had been bugged while he waited for her to finish dressing. She wouldn't mention that either.

"I don't know how you put up with them," Allen said.

"Because they are part of the surroundings for me. The only time I notice them is when others make a big deal out of their presence. We've been together for five months. You should be used to them too."

He grunted at her.

"What's wrong, Allen? You've never been this pissy about Eiliv and the others before."

"One of those freaks is going to watch us when we have sex, right?"

Meirion grinned at him. "If you're talking about tonight, you're being awfully optimistic."

"You said so yourself, we've been together for five months."

"Does sex have an expiration date now?"

"See? The idea of sex in front of those *things* bugs you

too."

"The Fey don't bother me. You're the one who's bothered. And I told you when we first started that I'm not ready for a physical relationship."

"I get that Eric was the love of your life and you miss him, but it's been three years. Have you even masturbated in all that time?"

This was not a conversation Meirion wanted to have. Allen knew Eric as a topic was off-limits. She decided to take a page out of the Fey book and not answer.

"Meirion?"

She stared straight ahead.

Allen sighed and shoved his hand through his hair. "Look, I'm sorry. I love you, Meirion. You may not love me the way you loved Eric, but I'd like to think you at least care deeply for me."

She looked at him but didn't answer.

"I'd like to have a physical relationship with you. Please. I'm asking straight out, like a man should. No seduction. No tricks."

"If you don't mind me calling out another man's name then sure. Let's go for it."

"Damn it, Meirion, that's not fair."

"That's my life. To answer your question, yes, I've masturbated. Every time I touch myself, Eric's hands are the ones I feel and I call out to him. The one guy I dated before you found out the hard way. I'm trying to spare you the same—myself as well."

"It might not be that way."

"Allen, can't we just enjoy tonight?"

He pulled into the parking lot in front of the club he'd mentioned and shut the car off. Neither of them moved.

Meirion could feel the tension and Allen's anger. She did care for him. The emotion was pale compared to what she had felt for her late husband, but it was there—unlike with her last boyfriend.

Maybe Allen was right and that would be the difference. She placed her hand on his arm and he looked at her. With a small smile, she said, "You win. Let's enjoy the evening then we'll have fun at my place."

"Why not mine?"

"One of my shadows will be there regardless of where we go." She pointed out the window at Eiliv, who stood waiting for them. Several people in the parking lot pointed at him and snapped pictures.

Allen cursed under his breath. "Fine. You know what? I don't care. If I can be with you, I don't care who's watching."

Meirion leaned over and kissed him. She laughed against his lips when he cursed again. "You really need to learn to ignore them, Allen. They'll be watching me until my ratings drop. If we have sex tonight, that won't happen."

Looks like Allen would see her underwear after all.

Chapter Two

"You're late."

Kiar didn't look away from Meirion and Allen when he appeared in the empty spot beside Eiliv. The couple nearest his entry location pointed and exclaimed in excitement. He ignored them as he was trained to do. They weren't his concern, only Meirion.

She was average height for her species, which put her a head below Kiar and the others. While her species named her black, Kiar would more accurately describe her color as russet. She'd gone through ten different hairstyles in the time he'd known her, even dying her dark brown locks red for a few months. The color annoyed her as much as it disgusted Kiar. She let it fade back to her regular shade and then let it grow so it touched her shoulders when she had it straightened. Besides, her brown eyes looked better when framed with her natural coloring.

"Our superiors detained me."

"Your human was worried about you. She's looked over here every five minutes for the last twenty-five."

"She isn't my human."

Eiliv laughed inside Kiar's head and the sound annoyed him. His outward appearance never changed.

"You should probably know she and Allen plan to copulate tonight. She consented during their drive," Eiliv said.

"I knew that already." It was the reason the superiors had detained him but he wouldn't tell Eiliv that.

The superiors didn't appreciate his enraged outburst when Meirion consented to Allen's suit. They spent nearly four hours reminding him of his duty as an observer assigned to Meirion. Kiar had listened with half an ear and waited for the lecture's end.

21

The threat of reassignment got his full attention. The superiors knew his weakness and they would use it against him if they thought he couldn't perform his duties properly. He'd apologized for his lack of composure and promised it wouldn't happen again.

Looking at Meirion, he hoped he could keep his promise. He may not be able to have her as Allen would tonight, but he wanted to remain with her.

When he first met the outspoken, somewhat foul-mouthed human, he didn't think he'd enjoy his assignment. Niets, the third observer, convinced him to stay for a few months with the stipulation that Kiar could transfer later if he still wished it. After a month with Meirion, Kiar didn't want to leave her side. A fact Niets teased him about at every opportunity.

On the dance floor, Meirion's hourglass curves moved in serpentine fashion with her back pressed against Allen's front. The man's hands cupped her hips and slid over her behind, hiking up her skirt. Kiar wanted to rip Allen's hands off.

Meirion looked his way, as though she'd heard Kiar's thoughts. Relief showed on her face and she smiled.

"*See?*"

Kiar didn't answer Eiliv's question. He watched Meirion staring at him and suddenly it felt as though she danced with him and not Allen. Her body moved more seductively and her partner didn't notice the reason for her change.

Yes, Kiar was sure Meirion felt between them what he felt. She'd never know he returned her feelings because he couldn't tell her—not through word or deed.

"Dude! It's a Fey. Quick, get a picture," said a man as he threw his arm around Kiar's shoulders.

Eiliv teleported before one of the man's friends could

23

embrace him in like manner. Kiar waited for Eiliv to reappear across the room then he teleported just as the camera flashed. The transfer took only a second but Eiliv had to go first so there would be no gaps in Meirion's recordings.

The superiors may edit out or time-lapse footage later, but Kiar and his cohorts had to supply complete footage at all times. The only permissible gaps were during Meirion's time behind a closed bathroom door. While the closed door was supposed to signal toilet use, all the observers knew their charges used the excuse to escape scrutiny.

Meirion had used the trick often in the beginning. The superiors had talked about canceling her contract when Meirion's adaptation time had taken longer than the others had. Kiar was happy when she'd stopped hiding from them as he'd discovered a growing attachment to her.

Twenty different households in the United States—a

few hundred around the world—made up the most watched television programming on the Fey home world. The network that thought up the idea of a human nature show had become the most popular and most watched.

Naysayers had existed in the beginning. They thought the humans would only react with hostility if the Fey returned to Earth as visitors instead of unseen observers. However, the network wished a closer perspective and for that the observers had to exist alongside their charges.

The humans had reacted with shock more than hostility. That could be attributed to the few times the Fey had visited Earth in its younger centuries. They were mistaken for gods and magical beings because of their advanced science. Though those few visits were few and far between, tales of the Fey had persisted through the generations.

While Kiar didn't mind the stories, Eiliv saw it as

another reason to disdain humans. The Fey of Eiliv's coloring—darks—were portrayed as evil, conniving murderers in human literature. Kiar didn't know where the humans got that impression since the dark Fey were the peacekeepers of the species. But then, the humans had many misconceptions about the Fey.

First and foremost being their actual name. "Fey" was what the humans called them because, at the time of their first introduction, the humans couldn't pronounce the actual name just a small portion of it. When they returned to Earth as visitors, the superiors didn't correct the misnomer.

Five years later, most humans were used to them, but there were still those few who found a Fey's appearance in public a surprising thing to be talked about in excited tones. Those few also tried striking up conversations with the Fey they found even knowing the Fey couldn't and shouldn't answer them.

The woman who had spent the last twenty minutes flirting with him, even though Kiar gave her no indication he reciprocated her intentions, was a prime example.

"*Enjoy. I shall see you tomorrow night,*" Eiliv said before he teleported. This time he would return to the ship and stay there until his next shift.

Kiar moved away from the chattering woman so he stood nearer Meirion and Allen's table. Allen looked annoyed at his presence while Meirion smiled up at him.

"You were late today, Kiar. Shame on you," Meirion said in a joking manner.

"I thought you were supposed to ignore them," Allen snapped.

"I generally do. But Kiar's never been late before."

"He's here. Whatever. Ignore him and pay attention to me."

Meirion took Allen's hand in hers and gave him a soothing smile. "Stop being such an ass about this, Allen. If it annoys you so much then break up with me."

"No!" He grabbed Meirion's hand in both of his and half rose from his seat. "No," he said in a calmer voice. "They're annoying but I can deal. At least we're back down to one again." He mumbled something under his breath.

"What?"

"Nothing."

Kiar had heard him. Allen wished Kiar wouldn't be there for the copulation. Kiar half wished that himself. He didn't know if he could watch his cherished Meirion with another man.

The superior's warning echoed through his mind. Staying near Meirion was more important than his jealousy. He relaxed his body. Over and over he repeated an old meditation rhyme his mother had taught him.

It promoted focus while allowing the speaker's mind to go blank. Not concentrating on the conversation would allow him to ignore it, along with everything else around him.

He moved when he needed to and followed Meirion diligently the entire night. His meditation failed him when Allen escorted Meirion home. Allen tried to slam the bedroom door on him. Kiar caught it, entered then closed it.

"Allen, stop that," Meirion yelled.

"This is still disconcerting. I'm not used to being watched while I'm having sex."

"And you think I am."

"I didn't say that."

Meirion crossed her arms and shook her head. "Allen, maybe we shouldn't do this after all. You aren't comfortable and I'm not ready."

Allen took Meirion in his arms and held her close. He whispered into her hair, "Yes, you are. This isn't just for me. It's for you too. You need to move on with your life." She looked up at him but he stopped her from speaking with a finger over her lips. "I'm not saying forget. I'd never say that. But it's time to stop mourning."

She nodded.

Allen moved that last little bit and pressed his lips to hers.

Kiar wanted to close his eyes. He could call Niets to replace him early and then make up the time later. The superiors wouldn't fault him but instead would applaud his foresight in handling what could result in a bad happening for him.

He couldn't do it. Seeing Meirion come alive in another man's arms would be torture but he wouldn't leave.

Chapter Three

Meirion wound her arms around Allen's waist and opened her mouth to his kiss. How long had it been since she let a man kiss her like this?

Easy. Three years.

Thinking the number made her remember Eric—her husband and one true love.

She tried to stay in the present with Allen, but the sensations building in her body wouldn't let her. Her body craved the touch of a man who would make her tingle all over with pleasure like Eric had.

Sensing the dangerous direction of her thoughts and what could happen, she opened her eyes so she could see Allen held her and not Eric. Instead, she focused on Kiar and his orange eyes. He watched in his usual stoic manner, betraying nothing of what he felt.

Meirion wondered what color a blush would be against Kiar's lemon yellow skin. Would it be red like hers or some other color entirely?

Was Kiar even embarrassed about watching Meirion have sex? He didn't act like it. She wanted him to be jealous. She wanted him to yank Allen way from her and take his place.

The thought bothered her but it didn't surprise her. Many times over the last few weeks, when she'd tried to avoid thoughts of Eric, thoughts of Kiar had intruded.

Meirion threaded her fingers through Allen's hair but it was Kiar's she wanted to touch in that moment. His green, waist length hair begged to be touched, to be freed from his ponytail and fanned out over her bed.

Allen's hand under her skirt jarred her back to the present and who really touched her. It was bad enough

32

imposing her dead husband over her current lover, but to do so with a living, breathing man who wasn't five steps away made her feel guilty. But her guilt wasn't for betraying Allen, but Kiar.

She backed away.

"What's wrong?"

"I can't do this after all," she said and backed up a few more steps.

Allen followed her, not taking the hint. He reached for her and she dodged.

"Meirion, this is silly. You can't let your memories of Eric keep doing this to you."

"It's not just Eric, Allen. I..." She shook her head and laughed at the absurdity of it all. "I can't do this with Kiar watching. After all the crap I gave you, now I'm the one who's uptight."

"You said you masturbated. Was he watching then?"

"No! I did it in the bathroom, sitting on the toilet. They can't watch me if I'm on the toilet." She didn't mention the sporadic nature of her personal sessions. The date of the last one eluded her, it was so long ago.

"I'll make you forget he's here. It'll be just you and me," Allen said in a husky voice. He cornered her between the bed and the bend in the wall and kissed her again.

Meirion squirmed free of his lips when he palmed her crotch. She pushed against his shoulders. "Allen, I'm really not joking about this. I can't."

He wasn't listening. He pushed his fingers into her through her panties. "So hot," he whispered then kissed her neck.

As much as she had anticipated this moment all night, she didn't want Allen touching her. His hands and kisses felt wrong. He didn't feel like a lover to her. If anything, he felt like a stranger.

She pushed against him harder. In a frantic voice, she said, "Allen, stop. Please, God, stop." He didn't listen. "Stop or I'll scream. I swear I will."

That got his attention.

Allen stepped back and looked at her.

Something made her move to Kiar's side, putting him between her and Allen. Kiar wouldn't help her since he wasn't allowed. Sure, if something ever happened to her, the footage Kiar and the others gathered could be used as evidence against the assaulting party, but none of them would step in and stop it.

Meirion didn't think Allen would assault her. Just to be sure, she reminded him of Kiar's presence. The angered look on his face said he comprehended the meaning of her actions.

"What is this, Meirion?"

"I can't do this, Allen. I can't. I'm sorry."

"Because of him." He gestured at Kiar.

Meirion looked up at Kiar then to Allen. She shook her head. "He's part of it. Allen, I'm sorry but I don't feel that way towards you. I thought I did, but—"

"You know what? I don't want to hear this. You and the creature from beyond the stars can go to hell."

"Allen—"

He stormed out of the room and slammed her front door.

Meirion sighed.

"I should have done it. My ratings would have skyrocketed."

She looked at Kiar for confirmation and got none. Looking at him made her guilt return. She looked away then stepped away. "I need a shower."

Washing away the feel of Allen's hands and lips on her body made her feel a little better. She put on her comfort clothes—big, baggy shirt and sweat pants—and sat on her bed with her photo album.

She hadn't touched it in years. The memories were too painful. Something had changed tonight. At least, that's how she felt. She wanted to see if the change was real or imagined.

With a calming breath, she opened to the first page. The first picture showed Eric sitting on a swing with her on his lap. They were mid-arc and the picture had a few little blur lines. She smiled when the cameraman's words of warning came back to her. First, he'd said she and Eric were too old to swing, then too big, and finally both of them on one swing might break the apparatus.

It had held.

That had been her relationship with Eric, going against status quo and propriety and letting what happens happen. When they met in college, Meirion thought she and Eric would be too volatile together. They argued constantly and came close to fighting physically.

One such close call ended with them in bed together. The sex was so explosive she and Eric were inseparable from that moment forward. She'd known Allen back then too. He was Eric's friend from high school and they ended up going to the same college.

None of their friends thought she and Eric would last, but they stayed together all through college. Eric disappeared for two years after graduation—no calls, letters, emails, nothing.

As suddenly as he left, he came back. He didn't have an explanation why he'd left but he'd apologized with a marriage proposal. Meirion couldn't stay mad at him and said yes. They were married the next day, which angered both their families. Neither of them wanted a wedding or a delay to starting marital bliss.

They'd honeymooned in Japan for a week then returned home. Eric bought Meirion a house—the house she lived in now—and spoiled her with expensive gifts. Her fear that Eric had fallen in with illegal doings prompted him to tell her the truth—as much as he could.

Eric told her, if someone asked, she should say he worked for the FBI as a paper pusher, but that wasn't his real job. He didn't tell her what his real job was or which governmental acronym he actually worked for. His secrecy scared Meirion and she made Eric promise whatever he was doing wouldn't get him killed.

He'd promised, but he lied. They had only been married for five years.

The military police escorts who accompanied the woman that had delivered the news of Eric's death while serving his country had to physically restrain Meirion from killing the messenger. She didn't remember much after that. She did remember tears and pain and empty sympathy from multitudes of people she hadn't known.

At some point, her mother and her best friend descended on her house and wouldn't leave until she ate something. Her life slowly got back on track until she was able to function on her own without people worrying she would take her own life. A few months later, the Fey arrived and started filming her.

She ran her fingers over the photo of her and Eric dressed in traditional Japanese wedding kimonos—she'd even had her hair done in the traditional manner. It was the closest thing they had to an actual wedding photo.

Looking at the photo and thinking about Eric didn't cause debilitating pain. Months ago, even days ago, she wouldn't have touched the photo album for all the money in the world for fear of sinking into a deep depression. The sadness still gripped her but it was manageable.

She closed the album and looked up at Kiar. A little thought fluttered in the back of her mind but she didn't let it take hold. Not yet. She had some things that needed doing.

The phone was in her hand before she realized she planned to call anyone. There was only one person she wanted to call, Tandy, her best friend.

"It's three in the morning. What the hell do you want?" Tandy answered her phone in a groggy voice.

"It's Meirion."

"I know that. What do you want, woman?"

Meirion smiled. "Are you awake?"

"No!"

"Then wake up. I want you to meet me at the cemetery." She listened to the long pause and counted down.

"What! What's wrong? Did something happen? I'll be

41

right there. Don't do anything stupid."

"Tandy," she said calmly. Her friend didn't answer. A heavy thump carried over the phone followed by Tandy's cursing. "Tandy!"

"I'm right here, baby. Please don't do anything stupid. Please?"

"Tandy, I'm not suicidal. Take a moment to calm down and get dressed. I'll be at the cemetery. Okay?"

"Okay," Tandy repeated in an uncertain voice.

"I'll see you there."

Meirion hung up the phone and changed into a pair of jeans. She debated changing her shirt and decided against it. Like Tandy said, it was three in the morning. Who cared what she was wearing?

"Looks like you won't be bored tonight after all," she said to Kiar as she passed him.

"Meirion!"

Tandy almost tackled Meirion when she hugged her. Meirion laughed at the woman's frantic state.

"Tandy, I told you to calm down."

"What's wrong? What happened? Are you okay?"

Meirion pulled back and regarded Tandy. The woman was definitely not at her best. Her sandy blonde hair was in a lopsided ponytail and she still had pillow marks on her face. The shirt she'd yanked on was inside out and her pants weren't zipped.

Meirion said with a small smile, "It's time to say goodbye."

"Goodbye! Why? What happened? It doesn't matter. We can work it out."

"Tandy, I'm not suicidal. If you don't stop acting like I am, I'm going to get pissed off and beat you in a bad way you won't like."

Tandy looked confused.

"I'm saying goodbye to Eric."

"Goodbye to…" Tandy gave a sad smile and hugged Meirion again, this time with soft understanding. "Oh, honey, I'm so happy for you."

Tears prickled the backs of Meirion's eyes but she blinked them back. She didn't want to cry. Eric had hated her tears.

"Why now? What happened?"

"I almost slept with Allen."

Tandy jerked away. She opened her mouth several times but nothing came out. With an angry grunt, she said, "I'm going to pretend I didn't hear that and just be happy you're moving on with your life."

"I said almost. It turns out Allen isn't my type."

"I knew that from the word go, but you're hardheaded."

Meirion faced Eric's tombstone. "That's what he loved about me."

"That's what he hated about you too. You two fought like you were the deciding factors in the gender wars."

"And we loved as though we had to repopulate the Earth."

"TMI!"

Meirion laughed. She smoothed her hand over the large slab of stone then bent and pressed a kiss to it. "I'll love him forever and I'll miss him every day."

"But?"

"No but. I'm not over it. I'll never be over it. Eric took a part of me with him when he died and nothing will change that."

"You're saying goodbye."

"To the pain. I looked at our photo album and could only remember happy times, not sad ones. That's what I've been waiting for—a time when I could rejoice in his life instead of mourning his death. I'm saying goodbye to that, not him."

"Does this mean you'll start dating again? Just not Allen, okay?"

She laughed. "No, I'm not dating Allen. He's fed up with me and the Fey. He didn't like me running to Kiar for protection."

"Protection from what? What did Allen do?" Tandy waved the question off. "You know what, I don't care. I'm going to castrate that bastard."

"He didn't do anything." She looked at Kiar. "Allen knows the Fey won't interfere with anything that happens to me, but reminding him of Kiar's presence made him back off."

"That bugs the hell out of me, Meir. What if you'd been alone? Would we be saying goodbye to your grief in a cemetery or would I be hunting down Allen with a butcher knife?"

Meirion hugged Tandy for that. "I love you."

"Oh! Does that mean you're going to give me a chance?"

"A world of no. I don't do women."

Tandy snapped her fingers with a mumbled curse. "You'll think of me if you change your mind, right?"

"I'll come to you first," Meirion promised in a bland tone. She gave the tombstone one last pat then turned towards the parking lot. "You know what, I'm hungry. What's open?"

"There's that waffle place down the street."

"You don't mind?"

"I'm up. I might as well feed myself and you. My treat."

The women walked arm-in-arm to their cars. Meirion glanced back at Kiar, who followed them. He was the catalyst to her change, not Allen. She knew that. Kiar was the first man to make her feel the way Eric had without her memories of Eric imposing themselves on top of him.

She didn't think it was her imagination that Kiar returned her feelings. Even though his expression was always blank, she felt something from him. She planned to find out what that something was.

Chapter Four

"Morning, Niets!" Meirion waved at him with a happy grin.

Kiar said, *"She hasn't slept."*

"I know. The superiors are curious how long the adrenaline high she's riding will last. Twenty-four hours without so much as a nap and she's showing no signs of fatigue. That is pretty impressive."

Niets's comment preceded Meirion passing out.

Meirion rose to retrieve a book she and Tandy were chatting about. She took one step then hit the floor. There was no warning.

Tandy jumped out of her seat and went to Meirion's side, upset but not surprised. She pronounced Meirion sound and sleeping for their benefit, then carried her to bed.

Kiar and Niets followed.

"That was close. You almost made an expression."

"You're supposed to be watching her, not me." Too late Kiar realized he should have denied Niets's words not chided him for shirking his duties.

"Unlike you, who only sees Meirion no matter what is happening around him, I can watch two things simultaneously. Watching you watching her is more entertaining than anything the superiors ever conceived. If they were smart, they would let you pursue your feelings and record the results."

Kiar wanted to clench his fists, but that would constitute showing an emotion and thus was off-limits. He lapsed into silence and hoped Niets would do the same. His wish came true for a time, but it didn't last.

Niets said, *"If you like, I could talk to the superiors. They haven't thought of the implications of a mixed relationship from a* ratings stand point."

"Be silent! Why the humans focused their negativity on darks instead of shades, I will never know."

"We shades learned to hide our true selves long ago. That's why we are in power and you lights follow us in confusion, trying to figure out how we got there. Darks have sense enough to let us rule while working in the background to temper our rash behavior."

Kiar chuckled mentally. "The arrogance of shades knows no bounds."

"Our arrogance is only surpassed by you and yours. No wonder the humans portrayed your kind as high and royal."

"Better to be portrayed at all than completely overlooked and forgotten."

"Isn't it time for you to leave?"

Kiar had won this round and didn't feel the need to gloat. He let his gaze roam over Meirion one last time then teleported back to the ship. Usually her sleeping form was reserved just for him, but the circumstances of the night before had dictated a change in her sleep schedule. Trading her sleeping form for her look of love and devotion to a mate long dead tempered his upset.

Watching her talk about Eric and remember her relationship hadn't upset Kiar or made him jealous. Ill feelings towards such a strong love felt petty. Niets wasn't wrong about lights. Those of Kiar's race liked to be above all emotions that could be construed as infantile or base. It's why everyone described them as arrogant, including the humans.

The shades were quite put off when they found out the humans didn't remember them in their tales, only lights and darks. Kiar blamed the shades' grey skin, brown eyes and black hair. They weren't as exotic looking as lights and darks.

Niets felt the same about the dismissal as all his fellow skin-mates—insulted. Though that insult hadn't deterred the deal the superiors—mostly shades—made with the human governments in trade for filming the human race unmolested. A deal they fully intended not to keep.

Kiar didn't blame them. Humans couldn't be trusted with Fey technology. But, they had years before the humans realized the Fey had no intention of giving them anything.

By that time, the Fey viewers should have grown bored with watching humans and the observers would be called back.

Sadness welled up inside of him at the thought of leaving Meirion for good. He fought the pain of loneliness every time he left her when his shift ended. He couldn't imagine leaving with no intention of ever returning.

"I'd like a word, Kiar."

He looked at Superior Trygg and repressed a sigh. When would they leave him alone?

"Of course, Superior." He followed the man to a quiet corner with concealed annoyance. A base emotion, but he'd give in to it just this once since it was justified.

Yes, his feelings for Meirion were obvious to one and all aboard the ship, but he had no intention of acting on them. He was light and perfectly capable of doing a job without letting his emotions get the better of him.

"You must be happy, Kiar," said Trygg. "The human returns your feelings though she doesn't know you have them."

"No, she does not. Her emotions are her own."

"They may be her own but you share them. I think that's dangerous. A one-sided infatuation is one thing, but you may forget—"

"You insult me, Superior."

"I have seen love topple the frostiest light's heart. I don't underestimate that particular emotion and you shouldn't either." Trygg put his hand on Kiar's shoulder. "I don't come to you as a superior, Kiar, but as a friend. Staying with Meirion because you wish to be near her will end your career, not just your assignment."

"Is this a warning, Superior?"

"If it will get you away from her faster, then yes, it is." Trygg dropped his hand.

Pride and excellence in his chosen vocation were paramount to Kiar, to any light, which was why he wouldn't let his emotions beat him. "I will prove to you and the other superiors I am capable of carrying out my job regardless of my feelings."

"This isn't a challenge, Kiar."

"You've questioned my integrity and my work ethic, Superior. To a light, it could be nothing else but a challenge."

Trygg regarded him for a while. His look went from worried to annoyed to blank. "Fine. If you would gamble with your career this way then I won't stop you. I've apprised you of the consequences."

"You have."

"Let me also add—failing in your assignment means you will return home. The network will not reassign you since this entire situation reveals poor judgment on your part."

"Thank you for making me aware of how dire the situation is. Though I am forced to ask, Superior..."

"Speak."

"Do you focus solely on me or have you given this warning to others, the participants for instance?"

"There are others, but they chose reassignment."

"They aren't light," Kiar guessed. No light would have

taken reassignment. His stubbornness wasn't only his personality, it was his upbringing. Trygg knew that and yet persisted all the same.

"No, they aren't."

"Thank you for your concern but it is misplaced, Superior."

"I hope it is, Kiar. I'd hate to lose you. Good rest to you." Trygg walked away.

Kiar entered his room. "Why are you here?" he asked Eiliv.

The man stood and said, "This situation with Meirion worries me."

"Not you too, Eiliv," Kiar said with an annoyed groan. He dropped onto a nearby chair and let his head fall back. "Why does everyone think my feelings for Meirion and hers for me are so dangerous? Surely a hybrid child isn't that scary."

"So, you do think of Meirion mothering your children."

"I didn't say that," he said, sitting up straight.

Eiliv smiled in a knowing way that grated on Kiar's nerves. "She is beautiful, for a human, and her personality makes her a joy to watch."

"But," Kiar prompted, knowing there was one after such a preamble.

"She's not worth your career."

"Bad news travels as fast as they say, I see."

"Be reasonable."

"I am!" He shot to his feet and paced the room. "How would it look if I took reassignment? I'd admit that I cannot control myself. The superiors are worried and a little doubtful, but changing assignments would give their suspicions credence and they would never trust me again."

Eiliv opened his mouth to reply but Kiar cut him off. "You will not convince me. Stop trying. This has gone far beyond professional concern."

"Lights aren't only arrogant, they are hardheaded, as well," Eiliv snapped.

"And darks are mistaken for being peacekeepers when they are really manipulating people from the shadows. The humans didn't misrepresent your race all these centuries, Eiliv. In fact, they saw what few of our people do and only after a handful of meetings."

Kiar smiled when Eiliv took several breaths in a bid to calm himself or articulate a reply—Kiar couldn't tell which. But, he'd won another argument. Today was a momentous day.

Eiliv said, "This isn't about race, Kiar. I shouldn't have taken the conversation in that direction."

"It hurts when someone ridicules your upbringing and heritage, doesn't it, Eiliv?" He nodded at the man's look of understanding. "Then you know how I feel now and you'll stop trying to convince me."

"We gravitate towards humans because they remind us of what we once were—constantly fighting amongst ourselves, trying to prove one race superior over all others." He sat then sighed. "I'm sorry, my friend. You're right. Giving in would only give the superiors cause to always question your work ethic in later assignments."

"Now will you stop bothering me?"

Eiliv laughed. "Fine, I will not broach the subject of reassignment again."

"Good."

"However, I do ask you to be cautious. Meirion doesn't understand what's at stake and we can't tell her. She loves her little attempts to make us talk or emote in some way."

"You enjoy them."

"I do, but she doesn't love me."

Kiar nodded, his mood turning somber.

"Be on your guard. That's all I ask. You've set out to prove yourself and I applaud your effort, but she is as stubborn as you, and just as determined." Eiliv walked to the door, but didn't exit. He said in a quiet voice, "I only hope your journey of self-validation doesn't end up hurting Meirion."

He left before Kiar could form a reply. Out of all the arguments presented to him, that last one almost made him concede.

His only thoughts were of his pride and what backing down would do to him. He didn't think what remaining in the assignment would do to Meirion if she mistook his forced stoicism as a genuine refusal.

No, Meirion wasn't weak. She'd try for a while then turn her sights elsewhere when he didn't reciprocate. She'd probably flirt with him with words and possibly touching—he prayed for touching. The most she'd done to date was use him as a prop so she could put on her shoes.

Would she kiss him?

Imagining her lips against his, even if he couldn't and wouldn't return the kiss, made his body tingle. The feeling pooled below his belly and he groaned at the pain of his instant arousal.

He wouldn't speak and he wouldn't show emotion, but his body would give him away if Meirion set out to seduce him with her body. The superiors couldn't fault him, since no male could control the functions of their lower anatomy given certain stimulations.

Kiar fell asleep wondering what her hands would feel like when they ran over his flesh.

"Tandy departed only minutes ago," Eiliv said to Kiar when he teleported to Meirion's bedroom.

Kiar knew that already. Part of his job as an observer

was keeping up with his charge even when away. That didn't stop Eiliv from giving him updates when he arrived or him from giving them to Niets.

"She's planning something. I've never seen her this quiet. She hasn't threatened to cut off my hair once since I arrived."

"And you find this upsetting?"

"Disquieting, not upsetting."

Kiar watched Meirion, as he was supposed to, and found himself struck by the same feeling of foreboding Eiliv had mentioned. Meirion hadn't greeted him or even looked at him when he arrived. That wasn't like her.

He'd scanned the footage taken of her during his absence and didn't remember anything out of the ordinary. After putting Meirion to bed, Tandy crawled in beside her and both women slept. Tandy woke first. She'd busied herself cleaning Meirion's house and cooking lunch.

Tandy's actions meant Eiliv had to start his shift early

so he could watch Tandy while Niets continued watching Meirion. The audience needed to know about the goings-on in the charge's environment as well as the charge themselves.

However, Eiliv's early start didn't mean he would leave early—another part of being an observer.

"*Ah, she realized you're here,*" Eiliv said.

Meirion had glanced over her shoulder at Kiar then looked back at the television.

Kiar said without a hint of conceit, "*She knew I was here the second I arrived. I think you're right. She's planning something.*"

"*Something that requires two not three, I'd say.*"

"*Even if what you are suggesting is her plan, you'd have to remain since my view would be compromised.*"

"*I doubt she knows that.*"

He wouldn't argue the point, since he doubted—even if she had plotted something for tonight—Meirion would

64

chance enticing him into sex when she didn't know if he returned her feelings.

She glanced back at them again then the wall clock beyond them.

Eiliv chuckled inside Kiar's head. *"She is definitely waiting for me to leave. Would you like me to go early?"*

"Do your job, Eiliv."

"Only asking in an effort to speed things along. This will be the night you prove to the superiors you can do your job despite your feelings."

"I can."

Eiliv didn't validate his statement and that made Kiar angry. He'd thought their earlier conversation meant the man was on his side.

"Nothing will happen," Kiar said.

Still Eiliv remained silent.

Chapter Five

Meirion almost cheered when the time came for Eiliv to leave. She turned on the couch and waved at him before he teleported away. As usual, he didn't acknowledge her farewell.

She stared at the spot he vacated for a long while, trying to make up her mind. Uncertainty kept her in her seat. Not about her plan. She fully intended to go through with it and without hesitation, but she wasn't sure how she should start.

A loud obnoxious car commercial blared from the television, making her jump. She hit the power button on the remote then stood. "No time like the present. And nothing beats the direct approach."

Long speeches and declarations of love wouldn't do it.

Besides, those weren't her style. Frank and direct were the words Eric had used when describing her. He'd also used stubborn, tactless and a host of other negative words during their few yelling matches.

When it was all said and done, her way got results faster. Besides, she wasn't interviewing for a job. She wanted to know if the man she loved returned her feelings.

After her goodbye to Eric, she allowed herself to feel the emotion she'd pushed to the back. Kiar made her heart flutter, her body heat and her soul sing. She'd only felt that once before and never thought she'd feel it again.

True love twice in one lifetime wasn't something to be overlooked. An emotion this strong wasn't hers alone and tonight she'd make Kiar admit it.

She walked into the bedroom, stripping as she went. Her body tingled as the moment of truth drew near. She faced Kiar and smiled.

"For the people watching, I'll be addressing Kiar for the rest of the night. Sorry if this is against the rules, but I'm not from your neck of the woods and this is my life. So deal or change the channel."

That said, she walked over, grabbed Kiar's hand and pulled him to the foot of the bed. He didn't fight her, but she knew he wouldn't. He and the others couldn't acknowledge or react, but she could still do things to them.

One of her games—once she got used to Kiar and the others—was moving the men around the room for what she thought were "better" angles. She'd hesitated at first, thinking they would fight her, but they didn't. That's when she learned touching for her wasn't against the rules.

She didn't plan to take advantage of that fact tonight, not anymore than she already had. If nothing happened tonight, she'd consider it for tomorrow.

"You know, Kiar, I'm betting you could mouth an

answer to me and the higher ups would never know."

No response, not even the one she suggested.

"Or, you could be a bump on a log for the rest of the night." She crawled onto her bed and sat in the middle. "For the record, you're the reason I was able to do what I did last night. I haven't visited Eric's grave since the funeral. I would purposefully drive the long way so I wouldn't even pass the cemetery."

Nervousness welled up inside her. She took a breath but held Kiar's gaze. Some part of her knew he hung on her every word. "I think I would have done it sooner if you'd been allowed to talk to me, if we'd had more than a one-sided interaction. But that's in the past and this is now."

She leaned back and opened her legs.

A credit to his profession, Kiar didn't even stand up straighter. A quick glance below the belt revealed he wasn't aroused by her display, either. That would change.

"This is a present from me to the man I love. I admit it and know it without any doubt in my mind. This is only for you, Kiar. Everyone else is just along for the ride."

It was her turn to watch Kiar. She didn't want to miss any hint that her admission or display affected him.

Kiar nearly swallowed his tongue when Meirion touched the bared flesh between her legs. Her declaration of love filled his heart. He wanted to do as she suggested, to mouth the words only she would understand, but didn't. He knew the rules.

No acknowledgment.

Meirion's reaction would give away whatever he did and the superiors would win. He'd expected her to talk to him and demand a reply or possibly kiss him, not this.

She spread herself wide with one hand and circled a finger from her other hand around and around her little nub. Her body quaked at the sensations she felt from that little contact, which made her breasts quiver.

Her nipples hardened and all Kiar wanted was to take each into his mouth as his fingers took over for Meirion's.

"Ah," she said in a breathy voice. "It's always nice to see a gentleman stand for a lady." Her gaze left his and fixed on his arousal.

That only made him harder. He, like the other observers, had adopted human casual wear. The zipper of the jeans bit into him and he enjoyed the pain while simultaneously wanting to relieve it.

No acknowledgment.

Meirion didn't seem to care. She lay back and opened her legs wider once she saw he wasn't as aloof to her actions as he pretended—and he pretended well.

The fingers that rubbed her nub slid lower and entered her body. She made a small sound of satisfaction then rocked her hips against her moving fingers.

Kiar seriously debated the pros and cons of sharing in Meirion's pleasure versus living with the shame of his failure and never seeing her again after he did.

Meirion was satisfied with Kiar's answer. Sure, any man would get hard if a woman masturbated in front of him—any straight man. But Kiar's arousal had almost jumped out of his pants. She didn't know men could get turned on like that. Maybe it was a Fey thing. Or maybe Kiar was that eager.

She'd bet on the latter and play to it.

She alternated moving her fingers back and forth, beckoning and then scissoring. Each motion was for her pleasure as much as Kiar's. As much as she wanted to touch her breasts, she kept her hands between her legs. She spread her legs wider still and pressed her flesh farther apart so Kiar would see every movement she made.

Anyone tuning in for this episode of her life would definitely get an eyeful. The thought didn't bother her.

Would Eiliv and Niets see the footage?

More than likely.

Would she act embarrassed when she saw them tomorrow?

No way in Hell.

They'd seen her do everything else, and sex was only a matter of time. She felt her climax nearing and held it back. This wasn't a quickie for stress relief or instant pleasure. She'd planned for an all-nighter. Her toys—she'd prepped them during one of her potty times—were waiting in her bathroom. She would use each one in turn until too much pleasure or exhaustion left her too tired to move.

She looked at Kiar and her whole body tightened. Her peak came with her arching off the bed and moaning deeply.

Kiar had gladly suffered through everything Meirion did to herself until she fell asleep. She didn't touch him the whole night, not once. That disappointed him, but he was thankful for the reprieve.

He lost count of the many times he'd almost lost control. The dildo she produced that matched his skin tone exactly had him screaming his meditation mantra in his head and praying for control. He'd wondered when she bought it if she'd only decided on gifting him with her pleasure the night before.

Her history with the dildo—more of a twin for his own arousal than Meirion would ever know—had him wondering how long she'd harbored feelings for him. The color wasn't a coincidence, surely. She'd mentioned masturbating during the times she'd hidden in the bathroom. Did she use it every time? Did she think of him?

The questions plagued him and he wanted nothing more than to shake her awake and demand answers. He couldn't. His duty to his career aside, if he touched her, shaking her awake wouldn't be the outcome. He wouldn't stop until he exhausted her a second time and possibly not even then.

"Morning, Kiar. Are you well?"

He growled mentally at Niets's words but said nothing in reply. He'd been in a state of erection all night with no hope of release. Even in sleep, Meirion's nude body sprawled on top of her covers kept him hard.

Niets's arrival meant he had one more hour to endure. Time seemed to drag in an effort to prolong his torture.

"Not talking, I see." Niets chuckled. *"Then, let me talk. The superiors are impressed, both with you and her. They've already come up with a special all night event so they can air the entire session in one*

75

spot. The anticipation polling numbers are off the charts."

Meirion's present to him was being used as marketing fodder to gain the network more viewers and more money. He knew it would, but the truth of it, the proof of it, angered him.

"The superiors also applaud your control in the face of such a temptation. I know a few of them sought private corners after only a few minutes of her display. I even—"

"Shut. Up." His words were as loud as he could make them. He'd almost said them aloud. Meirion stirred on the bed with a tiny mewling noise and he thought he had.

"Ah, the princess of the hour awakes."

Meirion stretched and opened her eyes, her gaze moving immediately to Kiar. A slow smile curved her lips. "Good morning." She stretched again then looked at Niets. Her gaze swept up and down his body.

Kiar gritted his teeth. He didn't want her looking at

any other man.

"Getting all hard and heavy over some other man's woman, Niets? You perv."

"Little harridan has nerve claiming to be yours when you've given no indication of your feelings."

Meirion approached them. Niets moved sideways. Kiar realized with annoyance Niets was making sure he could see Meirion and Kiar together. The man wasn't supposed to film Kiar, but Meirion's actions made it necessary.

She placed her hand on his chest and kissed the edge of his chin. "I'll see you tonight," she whispered then retreated to her bathroom.

He followed her out of habit since all cognitive function deserted him.

"Good rest, Kiar," Niets said, jarring him back to reality.

Kiar's time was up and he could leave. That was why Meirion had kissed him. He didn't reply to Niets's words, just stepped to the side so Niets could take his place in the doorway and teleported back to the ship.

No one awaited his arrival this time. He went straight to his room, stripped his jeans to his knees and grabbed his arousal in his fist. With that simple touch, his release came.

He dropped to his knees, breathing hard. "I can't endure that again," he said in a ragged voice. "I can't."

Chapter Six

"You complete and utter skank!"

Meirion slapped her hand over Tandy's mouth. "Keep your voice down, damn it."

Tandy yanked her hand away. "Why should I? Everyone already knows you diddled yourself on television."

"No, they do not," she bit out, looking around the room. She glanced at Eiliv then away. No help there. "Only the Fey know what I did—and you. That's it."

"Okay, okay. Don't get your panties in a bunch." Tandy sipped her drink. "It's a shame you wasted such a prime opportunity on Kiar though. I could have—"

"Don't, Tandy. I'm not in the mood for your jokes."

"What's wrong with you? I'd think you'd be happier."

Meirion sighed and dropped her head to the table. "I want to be, but this whole situation pisses me off the more I think about it. Sure he got hard, but Niets was the same way when he arrived. Maybe Kiar was just horny."

"He's a male. Duh."

"I'm serious!"

"So am I. You're hot stuff, Meirion. A man would have to be dead, gay or a eunuch not to get off on watching you play with yourself." She jerked her thumb towards Eiliv. "Was silver boy sporting mahogany when he showed?"

"No, but I was dressed when he arrived." She looked at Eiliv again, curious if he'd been aroused while aboard the ship. Not being able to ask added to her anger.

Her little display last weekend had definitely gotten everyone's attention, though not the results she'd wanted. The Fey higher ups in charge of the expedition sent her a thank you gift in the form of a new car. She wondered how they justified the car while keeping with their no-acknowledgment policy. Probably the same double standard applied to all people in power. Besides, the gift meant she could spend her car fund on something else.

While she was sure the network wanted her to put on her little show again, she didn't. She slept in the nude and touched Kiar at every opportunity but her night of self-pleasure was a onetime thing. If Kiar wasn't affected the first time, doing it again would have the same outcome.

She looked around the restaurant for something to distract her from her brooding thoughts. Seeing another Fey in the room shocked her a little. She hadn't seen another Fey besides her three ever. The people being observed were scattered, purposefully.

"Tandy, look, another Fey."

The woman turned in her seat. She looked at Eiliv then at the other man. "Well, damn. They could be brothers."

"You're only saying that because of his coloring. He looks nothing like Eiliv. His build is slimmer and his hair is to his shoulders."

Meirion studied the man, interested in the similarities and dissimilarities between him and Eiliv. One of the people at the table he watched pointed at her. She didn't take offense. It surprised her when the man turned and looked at her.

"What the hell?" she said in a loud voice.

The man smiled and she nearly fell out of her seat. He walked over to her, nodding to Eiliv when he passed, and stopped across from her seat. "Good day, ladies. My companions tell me you were curious about me."

"You talked," Meirion said in an accusatory voice.

"That I did."

"You're not supposed to talk."

The man smiled broader and sat down. "He's not

supposed to talk," the man said, gesturing to Eiliv. "I'm not held to such restrictions."

"Why?"

"I'm a participant not an observer. My name is Jor, by the way. You are?"

"You don't know?" Tandy asked.

Jor laughed and cleared his throat. "Let me explain real quick and then we can have a normal conversation. There are two types of Fey visiting Earth at the moment— observers and participants. Observers, usually in teams of three to seven, watch a charge. They are not allowed to speak or otherwise acknowledge their charges, only record them."

"Kind of living it, so I knew that already," Meirion snapped.

"Of course. Participants—such as myself—are even fewer than observers. We are a select few chosen to integrate ourselves into human culture. Our assignment means we aren't allowed contact with the ship or any of our colleagues."

"Oh! Will you be reprimanded for talking to us?" Meirion asked, concerned she might have gotten Jor in trouble.

"Not at all. It's a coincidence only. Don't worry about me."

Meirion digested the information Jor imparted.

Tandy didn't need an adjustment time. She reached out and thumped Meirion on the top of her head.

"Ow!"

"Hello, stupid! Jor is a Fey. A *talking* Fey. He can answer your questions about Kiar," Tandy almost yelled. She sighed in exasperation and rolled her eyes. "I'm Tandy, this is my best gal pal Meirion. She's not normally this dense."

"It's understandable. She's shocked," Jor said. "What did you want to ask me, Meirion? I'm at your disposal for—" he checked his watch, "—the next hour."

"What about your friends?" Meirion asked.

"I'll see them later. I may never see you again after today. We're roadtripping."

"So, you don't know what I did last weekend?"

"After such an interesting question, I almost wish I did, but no. I don't."

Meirion didn't know why his ignorance made her feel relief but it did. She reveled in the emotion for all of two seconds then put herself in business-mode. "What happens if one of my guys talks to me? Why can't they talk to me? Or react or something?"

"The same thing that happens to you when you don't do your job—a reprimand, a warning and eventually termination."

"So Kiar could get fired."

"Most definitely."

"I'd never see him again."

"Termination from the network means they would send him home," Jor replied.

"Oh God!" Meirion slapped her hands over her mouth.

Tandy asked, "What?"

"I almost...but I didn't know...and he...oh God."

"Complete a sentence, damn it. What the hell are you babbling about?"

Jor said, "I thought human females understood these half thoughts and incomplete sentences."

"Usually I can, but this is a new one on me."

Meirion said, "I only wanted to know how he felt about me, to show him how I felt about him. I didn't think I might get him in trouble."

"He's fine," Jor said, his tone leaving no room for

doubt.

"You don't know that," Meirion snapped.

"Eiliv told me."

Meirion looked at Eiliv then to Jor. "How?"

Jor pointed to his head. "Interpersonal communication network. Sort of like a cell phone for your head. Just like a cell phone, only the intended party can hear you. All Fey have one implanted at birth, allowing us to communicate without speaking."

"Like telepathy. Nice," Tandy said.

"This is plain old science, not magic."

Meirion asked, "So, Kiar is okay? He's not in trouble?"

"That's what Eiliv tells me. Kiar proved he can do his job no matter what you do to him, though Eiliv won't tell me what it is you did."

"Don't!" Meirion looked at Eiliv with warning. "I really will shave you bald if you do."

"Ouch," Jor said, laughing. "Such threats against a dark's hair. Do you hate him so much?"

"Is your hair important? Yours is much shorter than Eiliv's."

"Coming on this trip shamed my family and they cut it. It was a punishment, but it is growing back." Jor fingered his own silver locks. "As for the importance, we have a precious metal growing out of our heads naturally and through no scientific meddling. So, yes, it is precious. No dark would ever cut his hair and the threat of it is a grievous insult." Before Meirion could apologize, Jor added, "Eiliv understands you didn't know that and he doesn't want you to be upset."

"All I'm doing is making mistakes," Meirion said then dropped her head back to the table."

"Whatever," Tandy said in a dismissive tone. "While she's dealing with her own personal drama, I got a question."

"Listening attentively, Tandy."

"Where are all the women?"

"The female Fey stayed aboard the ship. From my understanding, there was a general uproar when they came planet-side so our government and yours decided our women wouldn't participate in this exchange of culture."

"Uproar?"

"Would you agree Fey males look better than most human males?"

"No contest, but I haven't met many of you."

Jor touched his chest. "By Fey standards, I'm average looking—plain if I was to be honest."

Meirion snapped her head up at that. "Bullshit!"

"You say that because you don't know any better. Suffice to say, it is true. The females of my race are much the same when compared to those of yours. And they tend to glow. The effect was too much for your men to handle and a few fights ensued."

"Glow?" Tandy and Meirion asked in unison.

"Their hair. It's not really glowing, but the play of light off their hair gives the illusion of glowing."

"Yours doesn't," Meirion said.

"My hair isn't gold. Dark females have gold hair, light females have blue hair, and shade females have white." He glanced at his watch.

"We're keeping you—"

Jor cut off Meirion, "Nope, I still have time. Any other questions?"

"Your women are so beautiful, then there's no way Kiar finds me attractive at all."

"Ah, but you have exoticism on your side, Meirion. And you are beautiful by human standards."

"Damn straight," Tandy said.

"Whoever this Kiar is, he'd be a fool not to return your feelings."

"He can't. He'll get fired," Meirion said in a dejected voice.

Jor cupped her cheek in his hand and leaned in close to her. She blinked at him in surprise, but his nearness did nothing for her. That made her feel relieved.

He said, "Lights are the stubborn, holier-than-thou race amongst the Fey. He's letting his pride stand in the way of his feelings, if he has them. I'd never let my job keep me from the woman I love."

"They'll send him away. What's the point of loving me if we can't be together?"

No, she'd already gone through that once, she wouldn't do it again. But, she felt her heart breaking. Kiar may love her but he'd never be able to show it or they'd be separated.

"Who cares if he gets fired and is sent home?" Jor

pressed a finger over her lips so she couldn't answer his question. "Even if that happened, he could return. The network isn't the only Fey vessel making trips to Earth. He need only petition to the superiors for a pass to return, then ask your government's permission—which they would be stupid not to give—to be allowed to stay with you."

"You're joking?" Meirion asked in a breathy voice. "That's all?"

"That's all."

"Would he be under surveillance? Would *we* be under surveillance? What about the camera in his eye? Do you have a camera too?"

Jor kissed her cheek then sat back. "I'm sure your government would watch him. I know without a doubt the network would insist that he wear a camera and possibly send an observer team, because filming such a pairing would be ratings gold. And, yes, I wear a camera. I have an observer as well, but my camera means he doesn't have to be with me at all times like yours."

He stood. Meirion and Tandy did as well. On impulse, Meirion hugged him. He chuckled and returned her hug.

"Thank you. Thank you, Jor. You've put my mind at ease," Meirion whispered.

"My pleasure." He pulled a card out of his pocket and pressed it into her hand. "Email me sometime and let me know how it turns out."

"Am I allowed?"

"Why not? I'm playing human and humans like to keep in touch via email." He winked at her.

Meirion got the feeling Jor wasn't supposed to do what he did, but he made a valid point. He was playing human. His higher ups couldn't fault him for stumbling across her and then holding a conversation.

Tandy shook his hand. Both women watched him return to his friends, who then left as a group.

"Now what?" Tandy asked.

Meirion glanced at Eiliv. Stoic as ever, but her inclination to make him talk was gone. She didn't think it would return since she didn't want to get him in trouble.

She whispered, "I'm sorry."

His blue eyes went dark, but that was the only change in his visage. Meirion mentally snapped her fingers. She'd forgotten to ask Jor about the color changing eyes. It wasn't a problem. She could ask Kiar when he talked— tonight.

She faced Tandy. Meirion made up her mind. All her sad and self-pitying emotions fled. "Now we take the kid gloves off. I'm done playing fair."

Tandy whistled under her breath. "That boy's in trouble," she said in a singsong. "I just wish I could watch."

94

Chapter Seven

Kiar reviewed the footage of the time he'd missed. He paid special close attention to Meirion's conversation with Jor. The man had helped him and doomed him all in one gesture.

Meirion understood his refusal to answer her, but Jor's suggestion for Kiar's return wasn't one he wanted. Losing his job wasn't an option to him. It would have been better if Meirion had spoken to another light who could have explained why Kiar didn't simply let himself be fired then return in another manner.

Pride, honor, integrity—those weren't just words to him. He'd promised he'd do his job and he would. If the superiors transferred him, it would be through no fault of his own.

If only he'd been there when Meirion spoke to Jor, he could have told her that, albeit through a third party. Jor's obvious disdain for Kiar's race had only served to make his relationship with Meirion more difficult. If Kiar ever saw the man again, he'd break his neck.

None of the later footage revealed what Meirion had planned for him tonight. She and Tandy went shopping, but Meirion had gotten nothing. Tandy had left to shop alone then returned.

Kiar knew Tandy had bought something for Meirion. Sending her friend to make the purchase ensured it was kept off camera and Kiar wouldn't find out about it ahead of time.

He looked at the clock and faced his upcoming time with Meirion with a sense of foreboding. Maybe she would add touching to her plan or maybe she would spend the night yelling at him.

The clock signaled time and he teleported.

Meirion stood in her bedroom with Eiliv *and* Niets watching her.

"*Why are you here, Niets?*" Kiar asked. Keeping the surprise off his face was a monumental task but he did it. He also kept his gaze on Meirion. She didn't look angry, only determined.

"*Based on a hunch, Eiliv summoned me. Meirion hasn't protested my presence, so here I stay,*" Niets answered.

Eiliv said, "*For the first time, all three of us will be needed.*"

"*You know what she has planned then? I didn't see anything on the footage.*"

"*I can guess and so can you. The superiors agree or they would have called Niets back.*"

"*Nothing will happen. Niets's presence isn't needed.*"

"Are you three done talking?" Meirion asked. "I know

you're talking. Now, at least. I'm grateful I met Jor. He cleared up a lot. Not as much as I needed, but I can always email him later." She looked pointedly at Kiar. "Or I can ask you?"

She would have to email Jor, because he wouldn't speak.

"We can do this the easy way, Kiar, or we can do this the hard way. It's up to you. Just talk to me." Her voice was pleading as she said the last.

He wouldn't be swayed. Meirion may love him but that love was without understanding. She wouldn't ask this of him if she did.

"*Talk to her*," Niets said.

Eiliv said, "*I agree. Even you are taking this too far. There are other options.*"

"*Not for me*," Kiar said in a growling voice.

Meirion stalked over to him and grabbed his hand.

"Fine. If you want to be stubborn, we'll do it your way. Just remember, I gave you the option."

She pulled him over to the bed. Subjecting him to another round of masturbation, while torturous, was bearable. He had worried over nothing.

"Last chance, Kiar. Say something."

"*Don't let her do whatever she has planned, Kiar,*" Eiliv said.

Kiar ignored him and continued performing his duty, as he should.

Meirion rolled her eyes then shoved him hard. He fell back onto the bed, unable to stop himself because of the unpredictability of her action. She snapped a handcuff onto his wrist and then connected it to the bedpost.

"I love you, damn it, and some feeling—women's intuition, gut reaction, whatever—says you love me, too. I'm going to make you admit it whether you like it or not."

She undid his pants. Kiar knew he'd like whatever she

did. He was already hard. But, he wouldn't relent...he hoped.

Meirion wanted to strip him completely, but decided against it. Eiliv and Niets had seen her naked before, so she didn't mind baring it all and did. She didn't know Fey etiquette in this matter, so she'd leave Kiar a little modesty in front of his colleagues. Since she essentially planned to rape him, it was the least she could do.

Besides, it wasn't really rape. He was willing, he just refused to say so—or give her any other hint.

She tried giving him another out. "I'd rather our first time not be this way, Kiar."

No answer. Niets and Eiliv changed positions. Eiliv stood near the head of the bed while Niets went to the far corner. One would record her while the other recorded Kiar. That was all the answer she needed. He wouldn't talk.

She faced the foot of the bed and straddled Kiar's stomach. Her anger dulled when faced with the proof of his lust for her. She took him into her mouth.

Today's episode rating would definitely warrant a few X's.

Gripping his shaft in one hand, she moved her mouth back and forth. She alternated between that and licking him. Since Kiar didn't take advantage of her position fast enough for her tastes, she moved her free hand between her legs and rubbed herself for his viewing pleasure.

She climaxed before he did. He didn't move or utter a sound. That didn't deter her. She maneuvered so she faced him. He was as blank and stoic as ever.

"I don't know if I should be in awe of your control or worried," she whispered before pressing a kiss to his unresponsive lips. "I'd think you didn't like me except this—" she reached between their bodies and gripped his arousal again, "—says otherwise. It's a little more honest than its owner."

With one hand she spread herself and the other held him steady as she sat back. Focus on her goal left her with a cry of completion. She hadn't felt something so right in years.

She didn't move. Her eyes were closed and she kept them that way to savor the feel of Kiar inside of her. Even with her eyes closed she knew who she was with. No other presence intruded on her awareness of Kiar buried to the hilt and throbbing.

His mantra was a jumble of unrecognizable syllables. It sounded more like screaming. The rightness of Meirion's warm depths went beyond his comprehension to understand. Despite the chaos in his mind, Kiar remained lucid enough that he retained control of himself. He hadn't moved. His gaze stayed fixed on Meirion.

He wanted to touch her, hold her, flip her onto her back and become one with her. None of it came to pass.

She moved, sliding slowly away from him then returning at the same speed. He thought she would talk to him or watch him, but the only sounds leaving her lips were gasps and moans and she kept her eyes closed.

Good. She wouldn't notice his orange eyes turning amber. Again, a bodily function he couldn't control. One connected to his strongest emotion, just like the erection buried deep inside her.

Her pace increased and he forgot how to breathe. Little by little he felt his control slipping. He fought to keep it even as he mentally shouted his pleasure.

Part of keeping his control was denying his fulfillment. The superiors would forgive his arousal but not his release.

Given these circumstances, they might overlook the lapse. He couldn't.

Every muscle in his body was taut. With strength of will he didn't know he had, he rebuilt the words of the mantra and recited them. Time lost all meaning and his mind focused, bringing his body more under his control.

His breathing restarted. He even managed to bring his heart rate down.

Meirion threw back her head and screamed at her climax. A warm liquid feeling surrounded his flesh and drenched his pants. If she'd done that earlier, he might have followed her with his own release. As good as it felt, he was able to hold himself back.

His precious Meirion looked too tired to continue. He was thankful.

Meirion opened her eyes.

Kiar still felt hard inside of her. She looked down at him and his stoic expression greeted her. He hadn't moved, not even to shift position beneath her as she rode him.

"No," she whispered.

She placed her hand over his heart. It felt normal to her—normal for a human, at any rate.

The happy tears she felt when she peaked poured down her cheeks in a flood of sadness.

"Kiar, please," she said in a choked voice.

His silence coupled with his lack of release spoke volumes to her when he wouldn't.

She was mistaken.

That couldn't be. There was no way she'd imagined the feeling. It matched the ones she'd had for Eric so closely she knew it had to be real. She knew Kiar must return them.

But where was her proof?

She looked at Eiliv. There was a telltale bulge in the

front of his pants. A quick glance at Niets proved he had one too. Suddenly, Kiar's arousal didn't feel as special as it had earlier.

The sensation of him inside her felt wrong. She slid off of him and sat on his stomach.

"You really..."

She reached for his face, but hesitated before she touched him. Her tears came harder. With an anguished cry, she covered his eyes and dropped her head against his chest.

Chapter Eight

"You proved me wrong, Kiar. Congratulations," Trygg said.

The man's words were genuine but there was sadness in his manner. Kiar ignored it.

"You proved us all wrong. It was stupid to question the integrity of a light."

"Your words mean much to me," Kiar replied, his own voice a bit somber.

Yes. He'd proved to one and all he could do his job despite his emotions, yet there was no glory in the accomplishment.

Meirion had cried against his chest while covering his eyes until her tears dried and only the sounds of her sorrow remained. After unlocking his cuffed arm, she'd fled the room and locked herself in her bathroom.

Niets had another five hours before his actual shift started, so he'd retreated to the ship. The man made no comment. He simply left.

Eiliv followed shortly after, leaving Kiar staring at a closed bathroom door.

It didn't stay closed. Meirion had opened the door to him while she showered. She never looked at or attempted to talk to him again.

Before she went to sleep, she stripped the entire bed and changed the sheets. She only had the one blanket set, so she'd pulled the afghan off the back of the couch and used that with a sheet and cocooned herself for the night.

Her alarm went off at five just as Niets arrived, but she didn't leave her bed. Instead, she called her office and told them she would be late. The conversation had been hard to follow since she'd taken the phone into her cocoon rather than emerge and talk.

When it came time for Kiar to depart, she was still buried.

Everything felt wrong. He'd proven himself at the expense of his love. If only Meirion knew what was at risk, she'd understand why he couldn't respond to her.

Such thoughts were little comfort given the circumstances.

Meirion pulled away when Tandy touched her hand. Everything felt surreal after last night. It was almost like it hadn't happened, except the pile of sheets and blankets she had yet to wash remained as evidence of her stupidity.

"He was aroused though, Meir. That's something, right?" Tandy asked.

"So were Eiliv and Niets. It means nothing."

"Meir—"

"Please don't, Tandy. I'm fine. You don't have to handle me with care. I'm not going to break...not like last time. This is different. Kiar isn't dead. He just doesn't give a shit about me." She pushed away her food with disgust. "That's not his fault. I was stupid for projecting my feelings onto him."

"I don't believe that for a second. You're not the type."

"Obviously I am. I embarrassed myself and probably pissed him off. Poor Kiar."

"*Poor Kiar*! Woman, if any more crap comes out of your mouth I will knock your teeth out. That asshole treats you like dirt and you feel sorry for *him*."

"Tandy—"

"No! You told me he loves you."

"He never said it."

"That doesn't matter. You are too levelheaded. You don't do flights of fancy. That's my department. I refuse to believe you imagined the feelings that let you finally say goodbye to your grief for Eric and move on. I won't."

Meirion felt fresh tears at Tandy's speech. The woman was her saving grace.

"It'd be one thing if this was Allen. Then I'd call up the guys with the straitjackets and rubber room to come get you. But this is Kiar." Tandy stopped. She grabbed Meirion's hand and held it. "Honey, you remember what Jor said, right? If Kiar is obsessed with keeping his job, then he would have to blow you off to do that."

"That's not comforting, Tandy. His job is more important to him than me. That's the beginnings of divorce not marriage."

"Okay. Before we start talking marriage and kids, could we maybe get to mutual first base?"

"No. Not going to happen. Either I'm wrong about what I felt from Kiar and I embarrassed him, or Kiar cares more about his job than me and I embarrassed myself. Neither scenario is one I find acceptable." She stood. Her lunch break was almost over. She'd already showed up to work late. Getting back from lunch late wouldn't go over well.

She said, "I know what I feel. It's not wrong and I'm not misinterpreting it. But, it's not enough. I gave it my best and now I'm through."

"Through how?"

"There is no way I'd feel like this again. Once in a lifetime is a gift. Twice is a miracle. Any more than that doesn't exist. I won't settle knowing... I won't settle."

"Kiar or nothing, huh?"

"Nothing. There is no *or*. Last night proved that. Cya later, Tandy."

She left before Tandy could continue the conversation. No amount of talking would change anything.

"*You aren't speaking to me.*"

"*What would you like me to say, Kiar?*" Eiliv's tone was annoyed.

"*You normally tell me the highlights of Meirion's day.*"

"*Highlights. Would you be referring to Meirion's missing appetite, her lack of concentration at work or her vow of chastity?*"

Kiar heard rising anger in Eiliv's voice. He let the conversation drop. All that Eiliv said, he already knew, but the man's silence disturbed him. Even Niets avoided him.

His other shipmates were both amazed at his control and angry at his lack of sensitivity. Only his skin-mates understood. They applauded his tenacity. That was little comfort given the reactions of everyone else—of Meirion.

"Kiar," Meirion said in a soft voice. She continued staring at the television. "I'm sorry about last night. It won't happen again."

"*How sweet that she thinks* she *should apologize, when it is* you *who is wrong*," Eiliv said. He teleported before Kiar could reply.

He was alone with Meirion. She sat on the couch staring at the television but reacted to nothing she watched. The food she'd prepared for dinner remained untouched.

The sight of her body covered in pleasure and the feel of her surrounding him as she took him deep inside her had no effect. Watching depression creep slowly over her did what nothing else before it could.

Kiar clenched his fists.

He thought seriously of breaking his silence and explaining everything to her. Loyalty to his duty as an observer didn't stop him. The sense of being too late did.

If he had spoken yesterday, given her some hint,

Meirion would have received him with happiness. After seeing her tears and hearing her apology, Kiar couldn't respond. She'd think he pitied her.

He let his hands go slack. This was a Hell of his own design. He'd live in it, but he wouldn't subject Meirion to his presence any longer.

In the end, the outcome was the same. He'd never see her again. The request for his transfer would be submitted as soon as his shift ended.

Chapter Nine

"Who in the—" Tandy did a double take. "Is it just me or did Eiliv get buffer?"

"That's not Eiliv," Meirion said, dribbling her soup from her spoon back to her bowl. "His name is Saehr. He's Kiar's replacement."

"Shouldn't he be watching you at night then?"

"No. I had the guys switch around. Eiliv took over Kiar's old shift and Saehr took his."

The soup looked and tasted horrible. Meirion pushed it away. Two weeks had lapsed since Kiar's transfer and her appetite still hadn't returned. She knew Kiar transferred because his higher ups sent her a letter explaining the new guy they sent in his place.

Meirion still couldn't decide if she should be insulted

at Saehr's presence. Tandy didn't see it yet, but once she got over Saehr's coloring, she would realize he looked an awful lot like Kiar. Saehr's hair was longer, dragging the floor, and he was a little taller but his features would make him Kiar's twin.

The higher ups hadn't just found someone to fill Kiar's shift, they were trying to fill Kiar's shoes. Did they really think she was so shallow?

Given Saehr's presence, the answer was yes. To prove how wrong they were, she'd asked Eiliv to switch his shift with Saehr. She didn't get an answer, but the following day Saehr showed up after Niets and Meirion knew the switch was made.

It really didn't matter who watched her at night. She couldn't sleep worth a damn. In her current state, she was the perfect candidate for a sleep aid commercial. If she managed to fall asleep, she'd dream of something unknown and wake up crying and unable to get back to sleep. Those were the good nights. Other nights, no position felt comfortable so she'd toss and turn all night, dozing more than sleeping.

"Meirion!"

"Huh?" Meirion snapped out of her thoughts and looked at Tandy. The woman had concern etched all over her pretty face. "I'm fine."

"You're not fine. Meir, take some time off and get some sleep. Get out of that house. Maybe it's cursed. Just sell it and start over someplace else with no memories."

"That won't solve anything. But you're right. I think I will take some time off. I've got tons of vacation and half of it is use-or-lose."

Tandy hugged her and she returned the embrace. "Honey, please snap out of this. Please. I don't know if I can handle another episode like the one you had with Eric."

"I stopped by his grave the other day. Someone placed fresh flowers. It made me think of his mother. I need to call her. I haven't talked to her since the funeral and even then I didn't say that much."

"That's an idea. Use your vacation time to get reacquainted with your family. Show them you're still alive. Hell, show them your new attachments. That should be great entertainment the entire time you're there."

Meirion disengaged herself from Tandy and stood. "I'm going back to the office to put in my vacation and sick leave and then I'm heading home. I'll see if changing the time I sleep helps any."

"Call me if you need anything."

"You know I will."

With a goal in mind, Meirion felt a little better. She knew her boss wouldn't mind. The man had already commented six different times on how haggard—his

119

word—she looked. He'd suggested she go home sick, but she'd wanted to work.

She delivered the news of her pending vacation and her boss had her out the door before she could tell him how long. He signed her sick leave for the day and gave her an open-ended vacation form. He only stipulated she keep it under one month and that she come back rested.

"I'll give Nancy a call once I get home to let her know I'm coming. She'll be so surprised. I hope she'll be surprised. I hope she's at the same number for that matter," Meirion said to herself. She got behind the wheel and started the car. "I should have kept in touch with her. Eric was her son and she might have wanted to talk with me about him."

Before Kiar, she wasn't ready to talk to anyone about Eric or even think about Eric. Now Kiar filled her thoughts with sorrow while Eric was her salvation. She'd laugh at the irony if she was capable of laughing.

She yawned instead. Getting home and taking a nap would do her a world of good. Staying asleep the entire time wouldn't be so bad either.

She eased into the waning lunchtime traffic, mentally ticking off all the things she needed to do before she could escape town for however long. The house needed cleaning. She'd let it go. Dishes from uneaten meals filled the sink, clothes had piled up since she'd resorted to only washing the outfit she'd be wearing the next day and the furniture had a layer of dust.

That she was able to think about doing something constructive with the intention of doing it meant her depression wasn't as bad as she'd originally thought. But, she'd told Tandy that already. Kiar wasn't Eric. The situation wasn't the same, therefore her reaction to it wouldn't be either.

Traffic slowed to a crawl. A few vehicles drove on the side of the road to the nearest highway exit. Meirion joined them. Traffic on the highway moved at a brisk pace. She'd be home in no time.

Everything went black a second after that thought. The last thing she heard was a blaring horn and screeching tires.

"Have you completely lost your mind?" Trygg yelled. "You brought her here. You brought a *human* aboard our ship."

Kiar ignored Trygg and paced. He didn't care about the consequences. At least Meirion would be alive.

The crash played over and over in his mind. It was all he saw.

He couldn't give her up even though he'd left. She haunted his dreams and watching the video feed filled the

122

non-busy parts of his days. So many times he'd wanted to go to her, but he'd held himself back. It was too soon. She wouldn't forgive him yet.

In between his meetings that morning, he'd gone to the screening room. He didn't like Meirion's tired appearance and her lack of appetite had him worried. Hearing her tell Tandy she would visit Eric's mother had given him new hope for the future.

If she could plan such an outing, then she was recovering. He'd stayed to make sure she stuck to the plans she'd voiced, dismissing his next meeting. The superiors would be angry but he'd planned to make it up later. Meirion was more important.

Kiar thanked every holy entity in every religion that he had stayed. He saw Meirion faint. Her body slumping over the wheel had sent her car into a skid. She'd caused a chain reaction Kiar hadn't stayed to watch.

He teleported to the scene. The domino effect still had cars ramming into each other. An SUV had smashed into the side of Meirion's car and sent it toppling end over end into the ditch between the north and southbound highways.

The amount of blood in the car had made him physically ill. He'd held it together and called for help. Eiliv and Niets had arrived a few seconds later. They needed no explanation.

All three men had worked to get Meirion out of the car. It was against all network policy and Kiar shouldn't have involved Eiliv and Niets, but he didn't feel guilty. The men had the option of not heeding his call. They'd come.

Once Meirion was free, Kiar had teleported her straight to the infirmary aboard the ship. The humans would have given her up for dead, but Fey technology wasn't so limited. Meirion would live.

He told himself that over and over and hoped it was true.

"If you think your transfer is going through now, Kiar, you are sadly mistaken," Trygg continued ranting. "This is against all network policy. If she was supposed to die, you should have left her to it."

Kiar stopped pacing and stared at the man. The expression he wore caused Trygg to back up a few steps. "*We* caused this. The Fey, not the humans. Our observation *changed* Meirion's life. There are so many if's I could list excusing my actions that you should know them already and speaking them is a waste of my time.

"Don't give me the transfer. I no longer care. My only concern nearly died today because of a fatigue and depression I caused heeding *your* rules. You should worry about your own life if the doctors can't make her whole again."

"You blame me? I gave you the option to get away from her. To end it before it went too far."

"*That* wasn't an option. And you aren't welcome here," Niets said in a low voice.

Trygg looked at all three men in turn then retreated.

Eiliv placed his hand on Kiar's shoulder. "She'll be fine."

"Why did you help me?" Kiar whispered.

"We didn't help you, Kiar. We helped her," Niets said. "Whatever ill repercussions may come of today, I don't regret my actions. You're right. The Fey caused this and we should fix it."

Kiar bowed his head. "Thank you."

"If you would truly thank us, don't make her cry again," Eiliv said.

"I can't promise that. We're both stubborn individuals. I can promise to make her happy to the best of my ability."

"That'll be enough then."

Kiar would have said more but the doctor exited the infirmary. All three men faced him with worried looks.

"She's whole once more. We cloned blood to replace that which she lost and re-grew the bones in her legs and arms. She's immersed in a nano-bath at the moment to speed up the cell regeneration of her muscles and skin." The doctor nodded to Kiar. "You were right to bring her here, Kiar. She would have died in a human hospital."

"Can I see her?"

"That depends."

"On?"

"Have you gotten your head out of your ass?"

Kiar stared at the doctor in open-mouthed shock.

"Don't look so surprised. I saw what happened, how you treated her. I'm not so sure I should allow you near her since your cold light's pride is why she's here in the first place."

"That won't happen again. You have my word."

"Do I?"

"My family's honor as testament, Superior. I won't make my same mistakes again."

The doctor nodded and stepped aside. "You can see her then."

Kiar rushed past the man into the infirmary. The nurse pointed him in the right direction. He entered Meirion's room and almost wept at the sight of her in the nano-bath.

She floated in a tube of liquid, unconscious. The nanites would repair any minor damage, inside and out, while supplying her body with air and nutrients. They were a true marvel of Fey technology.

Meirion would have no scars, no other remembrance save her memories of her near death. Once she awoke, Kiar wouldn't give her time to dwell on it.

"Kiar?"

He faced Eiliv and Niets.

Eiliv said, "The superiors wish to see us now."

"I—"

"She's a few hours more to spend in there," the doctor interrupted. "You should be back before she wakes. Go face your judgment."

Kiar nodded. So long as they didn't bar him from Meirion, he didn't care what they did.

Chapter Ten

Everything felt fuzzy.

Meirion opened her eyes and looked around. She didn't recognize the room or any of the equipment in it. The only thing that looked familiar was Kiar. He stood at the foot of her bed staring at her.

All she needed was a little less clothing and they'd have a repeat of her first attempt at seducing him.

"Why are you here?" she asked in a scratchy voice.

He didn't say anything, which made her laugh.

"Dopey me. I don't know why I even bothered asking. It's not like you'll answer."

"Actually, I have every intention of answering you, Meirion, but no idea where to start," Kiar said.

She sat up slowly, staring at him in shock. "I'm

dreaming," she whispered when her voice returned.

He rounded the bed and sat next to her. "No, you're not."

"Why are you talking to me?"

"I should have spoken to you when you asked it of me. I was an idiot who was more concerned with my pride than my love. I'm sorry."

Hearing Kiar admit it made Meirion remember she'd decided to give up on him. "You chose your job over me. I get it. I'm not upset."

"That's a lie and you know it. You don't understand anything about me." He placed a finger over her lips.

She stared at him in wide-eyed shock when he leaned forward and replaced his finger with his lips.

He said, "Jor only told you a half truth. The Fey have a long tradition of raising our children to perpetuate the stereotypes of our people's races. My race...lights are raised...*I was raised to put honor, duty and integrity before all other things.*

"The superiors accused me of being unable to do my job properly so long as I harbored feelings for you. I instantly set out to prove them wrong. I did, but it cost me something dear. My upbringing didn't prepare me for that." He smoothed his hand down her face. "I'm sorry I hurt you."

"And that's supposed to make it all better?" She pushed his hand away. "I doubted myself and my feelings. I thought I had raped you in a bid to prove something that wasn't there."

"Feel free to do it again. I quite enjoyed it."

"No, you didn't. You laid there like a lump."

Kiar laughed. His laughter grew when she glared at him. "If you realized what I had to do to stay like that, you would say I suffered right along with you." He pulled her against his chest and held her there even though she tried to get away. "Torture never felt so sweet. I held my control by a tiny thread."

"One I couldn't break."

He sighed. "Meirion, you have to understand what such a failure would have cost me. I regret the pain I caused you and wish it had never happened, but I won't apologize for my actions."

"I already knew you loved your job more than me. Let me go and get out." She shoved against him but he wouldn't let her go.

"You understand the importance of Eiliv's hair, correct?"

"Yeah. So?"

"A light's pride is held at the same value as a dark's hair or a shade's blood."

She stopped struggling and looked up at him. "Shade's

blood? What's so special about Niets's blood?"

"That's not important right now. My point is this—my pride holds the same value as Eiliv's hair. And like Eiliv's hair, if my pride is lost, it is readily evident."

"Pride isn't a physical feature."

"For a light it is. A light who loses his pride becomes dull—our coloring I mean. My skin, my hair and my eyes would all fade in color. Even my ears would droop. No one knows why lights react in such a way, but that is the price of lost pride." He cupped her face in his hands and met her gaze. "Appearing in public looking that way would shame me and my family. It would shame you. I couldn't subject you to that."

"I wouldn't care." She tried to hug him but he pulled back. His orange eyes darkened. She'd said the wrong thing. "Kiar, that didn't come out the way I meant it to. I'm only saying I love you for you, not your appearance."

"I know you love me, Meirion. And you wouldn't want to see me like that. Just as I hated seeing you depressed, because that is what the dulling is—depression."

"Okay. I understand that now. Okay? Don't be mad at me," she said in a shaky voice.

Kiar looked surprised. "Why would I be mad at you?"

"Your eyes changed colors when I said I didn't care."

"Meirion, that's not what that means." He kissed her, pressing his tongue past her lips.

She warmed to the kiss but he pulled away. A soft sound of protest left her and she tried to hold him close.

"A Fey's eyes show their emotion for the ones they are looking at. The darker the color, the more they cherish that person. The more they love that person." He kissed her again.

Meirion thought back on all the times she had stared at his eyes. They'd always been a dark orange. Always.

Then she remembered Eiliv's blue eyes turning dark too.

"What's wrong? You looked worried. I don't like when you're worried." He caressed her cheeks as though he would smooth the emotion off her face.

"Eiliv's eyes always go dark around me too. Does that mean he... I mean...he knows I love you, right?"

Kiar laughed. "Eiliv cares for you. He doesn't love you. If he did, his eyes would appear black."

"Oh. That's a relief."

She squeaked in surprise when Kiar lifted her against his chest then stood. "What are you doing?"

"I'm taking you to my room so I can make love to you. The doctor said you are fully recovered and could leave at any time."

"What doctor? Where am I?"

Kiar searched her eyes and she stared back at him in confusion. "You don't remember?"

"Remember what?"

"Your accident. You fell asleep at the wheel of your car and... Never mind. It doesn't matter. The Fey doctors healed you so you're fine now. You're aboard the Fey ship orbiting Earth."

She looked around again. That explained why nothing looked familiar. Her gaze returned to Kiar. He looked tense. "What's wrong? You're not telling me something."

His arms tightened around her. In a low voice, he said, "I never want to lose you, Meirion. Never."

He wouldn't say that without a reason. The accident had to have been horrible to cause the haunted look in Kiar's eyes. "I want to see it. I want to see the footage of the accident."

"No."

"Kiar—"

"No. You don't remember it. That's a blessing. I'll live

with it as my punishment for hurting you and that'll be enough." He walked towards the door.

"Was it really that bad?"

"You almost died, Meirion. If you had, I would have followed. I'm not as strong as you. I wouldn't be able to survive your death the way you did Eric's."

"I almost didn't. My mother and Tandy forced me to keep living."

Kiar smiled at her and kissed her forehead. "I look forward to meeting your mother."

Meirion was about to ask him what he meant, but he stepped into the corridor outside the infirmary and the clapping crowd rendered her speechless. Dozens of Fey filled the corridor, male and female. All of them clapped and cheered.

Meirion stared at them all in awe. The women had her undivided attention. She whispered, "Jor was right. They're breathtaking." She gave Kiar a sad look. "How can you love me when you have them?"

Kiar glanced at the women then back at Meirion. "Jor also said you think the way you do because you don't know better. While I want to hurt the man for his part in our problems, he said one true thing—you are beautiful. No other woman, Fey or human, has made me feel as you do."

She wound her arms around his neck and pressed her lips to his. The clapping grew louder. She deepened the kiss and Kiar responded to her.

Everything would be different from then on.

Epilogue

Meirion eased onto the couch with a groan. "This sucks. Why do I have to wait?"

Kiar knelt in front of her and rubbed her feet. "The doctors gave you the option of having the baby aboard the ship. You turned them down."

"I didn't want to spend my last trimester cooped up on that stupid ship. You may like it up there, but I don't."

"And this is the consequence of your dislike, my love." He laughed when she kicked him. "The doctors won't chance teleporting you this late in your pregnancy. You have to wait for the baby to be ready and have it in a human hospital." He wrinkled his nose at the last.

"See? You don't want me to have the baby here anymore than I do."

"A Fey doctor will be in attendance. That eases my worry a bit."

She smoothed her hands over her large belly. In a few more days, she'd be holding the newest addition to her family—Kiar's daughter, the first human-Fey hybrid.

"*Rather than worrying about when your labor will start, you should worry about how many people will be in attendance. From what I've gathered, it will rival the crowd at your wedding,*" Niets said.

Meirion groaned. "Why did you remind me? I feel like a circus freak."

Kiar and Meirion had married a year ago. The entire event—the first human-Fey marriage—was a multi-billion dollar production from beginning to end. Dignitaries from all over Earth and the Fey home world had attended, along with every news crew in existence. They'd barely had room for their families and friends.

The exchanging of vows had taken three minutes while the entire ceremony had taken twelve hours because of the speeches and choreographed dance numbers. The wedding party had to be convinced, under penalty of both human and Fey law, to attend the reception.

Meirion had almost gotten Kiar to chance it, but they'd conceded and went. The party ended when Meirion had passed out from exhaustion. Kiar had told her everyone was frantic, but he'd never been happier for her little idiosyncrasy. It had allowed them to retreat to the ship where they'd spent a blissful week alone, except for Eiliv and Niets.

"Niets exaggerates. Both our governments want the baby to be born healthy and happy so they won't chance upsetting the mother during her labor with crowds and commotion. You'll be fine, Meirion," Eiliv said.

She smiled at him. He stood in the far corner of the

room looking stoic. She didn't mind since she could hear him speak.

The network had changed their policy on how the observers performed their jobs. All those under observation were fitted with their own interpersonal communication device so their "cameramen" could talk to them without compromising the no-acknowledgment policy. The viewers couldn't hear the conversation and wouldn't know unless the observee answered aloud to a comment the observer made.

While they were cautioned to keep the conversations to a minimum so as not to taint the illusion of watching a real human's life unfold, Kiar's presence at her side made Meirion's case an exception.

Kiar had been switched to participant status after her accident. Though the men received a stern talking to for helping her, none of them had gotten punished. Eiliv and

Niets remained her observers with the addition of two others, who only took over when Eiliv and Niets were tired or needed a break. Otherwise, the men were with them constantly.

To Meirion, they were one big happy family, so she didn't mind their presence. Hell, they had been there when the baby was conceived. She smiled at that memory.

Kiar kissed her lips. "What are you thinking about?"

"How happy I am that I met you." She looked at Eiliv and Niets in turn. "All of you."

The doorbell rang and then Tandy walked through the door. She smiled at them. "How's my little Mommy-to-be doing today?"

A Fey female of shade coloring followed her. Meirion smiled at the woman, happy that Tandy had finally found someone of her own to love.

Kiar answered, "Mommy-to-be is grumpy and

144

complaining as usual, Tandy."

"You should have stayed on the ship." She looked at her companion. "Right?"

The woman nodded.

Meirion snapped, "Oh shut up. Shoulda, coulda, woulda won't help me right now. This is—oh!" She clutched her stomach and sat up straight. Everyone looked at her with concern, even Eiliv and Niets. She'd tease them about emoting later. "I think it's time."

Kiar scooped her into his arms and marched out of the house. By the time he made it to the curb, an ambulance had pulled up and the medics jumped out to take charge of Meirion. A Fey doctor appeared next to the vehicle.

Sirens blared as police cruisers arrived followed by a few news crews.

Meirion groaned. "This is going to be a circus."

"All part of loving me," Kiar said.

"Which is the only reason I put up with it."

The End

HOMEPAGE URL:

http://dreneebagby.com

or

http://zenobiarenquist.com

Zenobia Renquist (Zen-Ren) is the pseudonym of D. Reneé Bagby. Zen-Ren was invented with the intention of keeping Reneé's Multiverse stories separate from her stand alone stories, thus cutting back on confusion (both hers and the readers').

Reneé is still fairly new to the publishing world but she loves to write and does so at every opportunity. When she isn't writing (because she's at her day job or otherwise away from her computer), Reneé is thinking up stories and characters to write about.

She hopes to have all her story ideas published one day and that they will be enjoyed. Visit her website at http://dreneebagby.com / http://zenobiarenquist.com or join her Yahoo! Group http://groups.yahoo.com/group/dreneebagby_multiverse/ to learn more about Reneé and her works.

More tempting books out:

Zenobia Renquist

Free Reads

Dare or Consequences
The Tigers and the Twenty-Nine
Forever Lovers

Red Rose Publishing

Acknowledging Meirion

(writing as) D. Reneé Bagby

Samhain Publishing

Adrienne (Bron Universe)

Serenity (Gezane Universe)